THIS WALKER BOOK BELONGS TO:

_____   _____

_____

_____

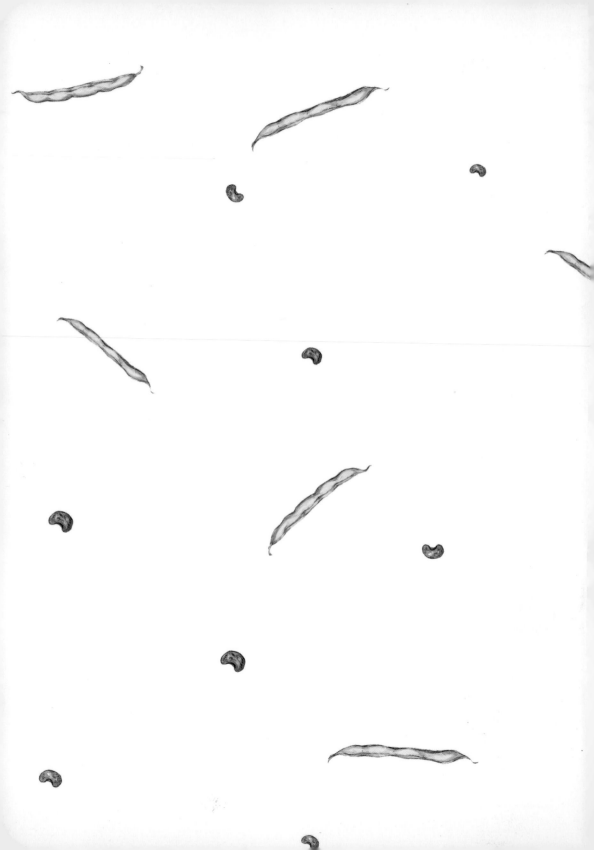

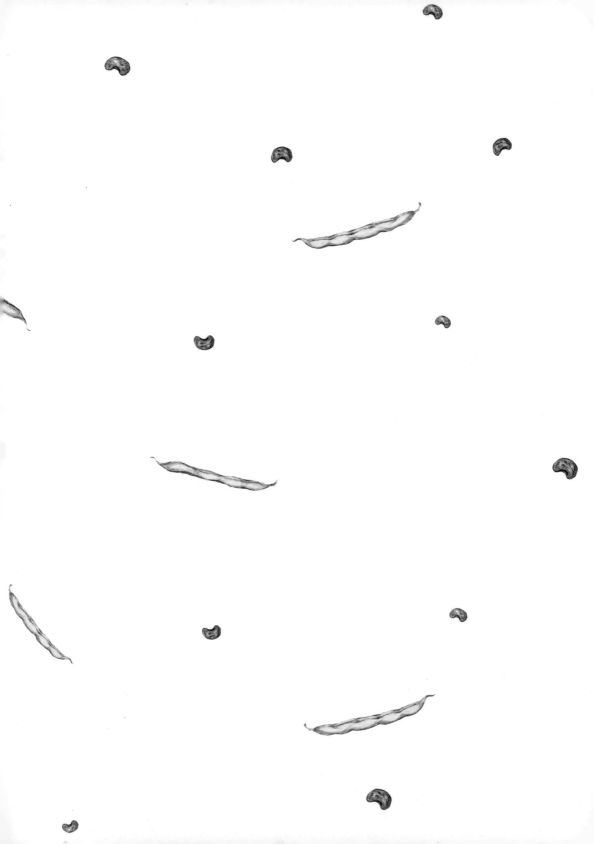

For Liz, with all my love
M.J.D.

With thanks to Walker Books
J.A.

First published 1999 by Walker Books Ltd,
87 Vauxhall Walk, London SE11 5HJ

This edition published 2006

2 4 6 8 10 9 7 5 3 1

Text © 1999 Malachy Doyle
Illustrations © 1999 Judith Allibone

The right of Malachy Doyle and Judith Allibone to be identified as
author and illustrator respectively of this work has been asserted by them
in accordance with the Copyright, Designs and Patents Act 1988

This book has been typeset in Usherwood

Printed in China

British Library Cataloguing in Publication Data:
a catalogue record for this book is available from the British Library

ISBN 1-4063-0026-8

www.walkerbooks.co.uk

JODY'S BEANS

Malachy Doyle

illustrated by Judith Allibone

WALKER BOOKS
AND SUBSIDIARIES

LONDON · BOSTON · SYDNEY · AUCKLAND

It was springtime, and Jody's Granda
came to visit.

He brought Jody a packet of runner beans.

They counted them out on
the kitchen table.

"...nine, ten, eleven, twelve," said Granda.

"That's enough."

They went out into the garden and found

the sunniest spot where the wind never blew.

They dug the soil and pulled out

all the weeds, mixed in some compost

and raked it over.

Then Jody made twelve holes in a circle,

and put one seed in each.

"Don't forget to
water them, Jody,"
said Granda.

"What do runner beans look like,
Granda?" asked Jody.

"Wait and see,"
said Granda.
"Wait and see."

The next few weeks were hot.

The sun burned down on the garden.

Jody watered her plants every day.

They snaked up the wigwam,

hooking themselves on to the string

as they went.

"Granda," she said on the phone,
"they're bigger than me now!"

"That's great, Jody,"
said Granda.

"How big will
they get?"
Jody asked.

"Wait and see," said Granda.
"Wait and see."

After the warm
sunny days returned
the first beans
appeared.

The plants reached the
tops of the poles, and Granda
came to visit again.

"They're even taller
than you, Granda!"
said Jody.

"They're wonderful beans, Jody,"
Granda said, pinching the tips at the
tops of the poles. "You must have green
fingers, just like your Granda."

"Will the baby have green fingers
too, Granda?" asked Jody.

"Wait and see,"
said Granda.
"Wait and see."

"It's time to find out what they
taste like," said Granda.

"Oh," said Jody,
"I didn't know we
were going to eat them."

So Jody and Granda picked handfuls
of long thin green beans.

They topped
and tailed them,

sliced and boiled them,

and served them up with butter.

"Mmm!" said Mum. "They're delicious."

The beans grew on and on,

right into the autumn.

Jody picked them every day.

If she missed one, it grew hard and knobbly.

Mum had to cut the stringy edges off.

It didn't taste as nice.

At the end of autumn Granda and Jody
picked the very last beans.

They were the ones right up
at the top of the poles
where Jody couldn't reach.

They were gigantic!

26

"They're no good,"
said Jody sadly.

"Oh yes they are,"
said Granda.

And he opened them up,

took out the seeds, and spread

the twelve biggest

ones in a circle on

the kitchen table.

"Do you know what these are for, Jody?"
he asked.

"Yes, Granda," said Jody, smiling.

"They're next year's runner beans!"

"And how tall do you think they'll grow?"
asked Granda.

"Wait and see,
Granda,"
said Jody.
"Wait and see."

Index

Look up the pages to find out
about all these bean things.

About the Author

Malachy Doyle lives on the west coast of Wales,
between the mountains and the sea — where, he says,
he grows plants, cats and teenagers.
His favourite sight in the garden is the runner beans
in full flower — a mass of bright scarlet, with the
prospect of tasty meals to come. He recommends
frying the smallest, tenderest beans you can find in
butter and garlic — delicious!

About the Illustrator

Judith Allibone drew inspiration for the white cat in this
story by watching a neighbour's cat playing in the
vegetable patch at the bottom of her garden.
Her own cat is called Myrtle May and
it's black-and-white. This is Judith's first picture book,
and she says that she hopes it will encourage
children to grow things.